He Smiled to Himself
(as recorded by The Old Man)

Steve Sanfield

Illustrations by Jeannie Kamins

Shakti Press—Berkeley

copyright © Steve Sanfield 1990

40 Days and 40 Nights was originally published in 1983 in a slightly different version by Plain View Press, Austin, Texas as a limited, signed edition.

All rights reserved. No part of this book may be reproduced in any form without permission in writing of the publisher, except by a reviewer who wishes to quote brief passages in connection with a review written for inclusion in a magazine or newspaper. Printed in the United States of America.

Design by Brenn Lea Pearson
Typesetting by ATypical, Ink

Shakti Press
P.O. Box 310
North San Juan, CA 95960

ISBN 0-933211-01-5

for Sarah

初夢や
秘めてかたらず
一人笑む

*The year's first dream.
Kept it a secret
and smiled to myself.*

—*Sho-ū*

I

40 Days and 40 Nights

*When your demon is in charge
do not try to think consciously.
Drift, wait, and obey.*

—Rudyard Kipling

Said what had to be said.
Did what had to be done.
Just wishes he felt better.

Their final night together
filled with declarations
each know to be false.

Holding on / giving up
    the same
Silence is its own music.

Wearing his father's undershirts
and his son's stretched-out socks
　as much from choice as need
he finally becomes The Old Man.

Just to make her jealous
went out and got his back
all scratched up.
She didn't even come.

The flowers he picked for her
have begun to fade.
This time he won't replace them.

On nights like these
he's sure he's made
a terrible mistake.

What a beautiful song it was
but The Old Man's too drunk
to ever bring it back.

Sure he thinks of her everyday.
What the hell
a man's got to think about something.

The Old Man just lies there
—a pile of dirty laundry
waiting to be washed.

Taught the hopelessness
of it all by one
he now waits for another.

Behind every laugh
the ghost of the one
not there.

The next morning she said:
It wasn't The Old Man
who made love to me last night.

Once she was.
Now she isn't.
Today he settles for this.

Cleaning house.
Poems scattered
everywhere.

Reading his old poems
he sees
—even then.

Regretting nothing done.
Only that
which was not.

Fame / riches?
Came close a few times.
Now only a chapter
in some misplaced book.

The Old Man gets drunk.
Embarrasses everyone
except himself.

Even without
a few drinks
he acts that way.

He suspects he's going mad
composing letter after letter
trying to explain it all.

Business or pleasure? she asks.
It's all the same to me he says
and suddenly there's nothing left
to talk about.

Other bodies.
The cock rises.
The heart remains still.

The Old Man goes dancing.
Finds out he really is
The Old Man.

Sleep on the couch she says
cutting his fantasies
in two.

The Old Man remembers
beginning to masturbate.
Can't recall if he finished.

He knows he's written
songs of glory
but he can't seem to find
a single one.

Though neither one works
he continues to reach
for bottle and pen.

Morning clouds suggest
work to be done.
He chooses to ramble
the woods instead.

Forty days and forty nights
   no better   no worse
Just forty days and forty nights.

envoi

He never said what wilderness it was
Where he spent the forty days. . .

—Haniel Long

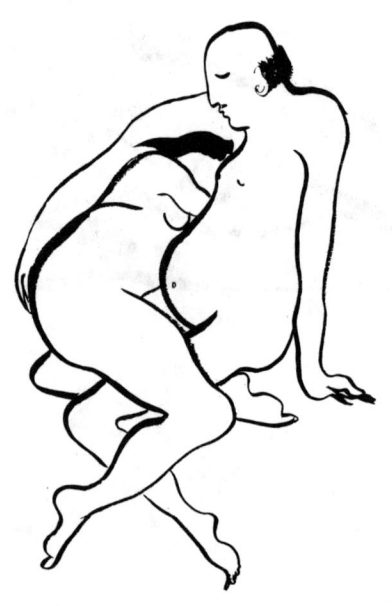

II

It's Come To This

*The good gets better
and the bad gets worse.*

—Mose Allison

A new season.
Not much to show
for the last.

The first narcissus
and his nose
all stuffed up.

Claims he doesn't care
but he does.
He does.

Too drunk at night
but always ready in the morning.
She's very patient.
He's very grateful.

Doesn't really matter
who shares their beds.
She's there.
He's here.

The Old Man said *No*.
His poems say *Yes*.
Some confusion here.

Knowing he could go to her
at any moment
only makes it worse.

What he did tonight
was
not call her.

So confused
he screams
even at the crickets.

His white legs tell him
how deep into winter
he really is.

Each day
waking to the fact
he must begin again.

Women everywhere
but The Old Man ends up
dancing with a balloon.

He thinks it's him
until his friend says:
*She puts out a space
we all want to fill.*

With no one to please
The Old Man becomes
fat and shabby.

Caught in a mirror
he understands what happened
to Marlon and Orson.

Finally gets a check
for his poetry.
Burns it with the trash.

Buys a new glass to celebrate.
Breaks it even before
he can pour a drink.

Puts in a new ribbon.
Mispells
the first word.

More and more
sure of
less and less.

Surrounded by beautiful bodies
The Old Man comes to love
his own.

One passion to another:
   agony   delight
Both require equal time.

Emptying the chamber pot
he notices the moon
pours it on himself.

Taking vitamins
to stay alive.
Some life.

Other men's women
would drive him crazy
if he let them.

This one mends his clothes
makes pies and cobblers
offers her beauty and body.
He wants to want her.

Gone so far
even the loving
can't heal it.

The fantasies of years
there for the taking.
Who is it that cares?

The Old Man sends himself
a welcome home card.
It never arrives.

Not the size or shape
of the window
but what it lets you see.

For the first time
not counting
—the last time.

Left so much behind
The Old Man feels like a traitor
though he's not sure to what.

Rain on the roof.
A cricket in the house.
As it is.

III

Could This Be Paradise?

*There is a difference between learning
one's lesson a hundred times
and learning it one hundred and one.*

—Talmud

Setting off again.
No direction.
Just gone.

Three days out:
one flat   two new tires
broken oil pan   lost sleeping bag.
So far so good.

All night—

beginning with one kind of fear

ending with another.

The next morning
The Old Man feels so young
he has Sugar Pops for breakfast.

Sinking deeper but
he doesn't care.
He's enjoying himself.

Her body so beautiful
The Old Man resolves to do
something about his own.

Seems like a dream
except
for the bites.

The sun
burns her marks
deeper.

Any dreams left?
Oh yes he answers.
If only I could get
my typewriter cleaned.

Getting used to
returning to
an empty house.

That cricket he rescued
from the dishwater
kept him awake all night.

A full desk
and empty woodshed
pull with equal force.

Love poems
scribbled for one
now sent to another.

Never before
these aches that can't be
blamed on anything.

Obsessed with it
he writes still another
about snow and almond blossoms
falling together.

Goes exploring
a fantasy of the mind
in the flesh.

The night before
like a child
waiting for his birthday.

. . . by refrigerator light
her bending body
through a new kimono . . .

Each time
surprised by it:
beauty beyond desire.

Can't remember
what he came for.
Whatever it was
got a good start on it.

Reading her a love poem
The Old Man stops
to answer the phone.

The act
new every time.
Praise the mystery.

Try as he may
finds nothing wrong
so he goes on.

It all ripens
along with
the blackberries.

With her away
The Old Man delights in
washing her clothes.

It all gets done
spoken with the luxury
of not remembering
he's almost fifty.

The Old Man feels so good
he doesn't even want
to speak about it.

The loudest sound:
the quail
at dawn.

Also by Steve Sanfield

Poetry: Water Before and Water After
Backlog
A Fall From Grace
Wandering
A New Way

Translation: Only the Ashes— Kage

Folklore: The Confounding— A Paiute Tale To Be Told Aloud

A Natural Man— The True Story of John Henry

The Adventures of High John the Conqueror

Recordings: Singing Up The Mountains
Could This Be Paradise?